Nick, Jess and Mum put all the boxes in
the cellar. Later, Nick and Jess went down
to find Nick's things.

The cellar was dark and cold.

"Good thing I brought my torch," said Jess, shining it around the room. "Your cellar is much smaller than mine."

"I don't like this place," said Nick. "It's creepy."

Nick tried to look into a box, but it was so dark he knocked it over. Mum's papers and pens fell all over the floor.

One of the pens rolled away and fell between two floorboards. It vanished into the darkness below.

"No!" cried Nick. With a sinking feeling, he looked through a crack in the floorboards. "That's Mum's best pen! Now it's lost forever!"

"Maybe not," said Jess. "Let's pull up the floorboards and try to reach it."

They lifted three floorboards, and Jess shone
the torch down into the darkness. Underneath
the floorboards, there was more of the cellar.

"That's why your cellar is smaller than mine," said
Jess. "Half of it's covered up. Let's have a look!"

Nick looked at her as if she was mad. "Let's not.
It's even creepier down there."

But Jess had already climbed through the gap in the floorboards. She wanted to solve the mystery.

Nick sighed and followed her. He wasn't so keen on solving the mystery.

The lower half of the cellar was dark and dusty.
It smelt like old socks.

"I can't see Mum's pen," said Nick.
"Shine the torch over here."

Jess shone the torch at the floor beside Nick.
"Here it is!" he said, picking it up.

The torch light also showed a huge hole in the floor, right next to Nick. When he saw it, he gave a yelp of surprise and dropped the pen. It fell into the hole, and they heard it going down and down.

Clunk ... clatter ... clunk ...

"Look at these shovels, and this old oil lamp,"
said Jess, swinging the torch around the rest
of the cellar. "Someone was digging down here
long ago, and then they covered up half the cellar.
I wonder why?"

"Never mind that," said Nick, "The pen has *really* gone forever now."

"Do you think they found something?" asked Jess, who wasn't listening. "Something that scared them?"

Suddenly, a strange growl came from deep under the hole. Nick's hands started to shake.

"Yes, I think they found something that scared them!" Nick said.

The growl got louder and louder.
Suddenly, the head of a huge, slimy monster
poked out of the hole.

Nick screamed. Jess screamed. The monster growled.

Terrified, Nick and Jess backed away from the hole. They scrambled up through the gap in the floorboards and ran as fast as they could.

The monster crawled out of the hole, roaring and growling. It held Mum's pen in its claw.

Nick and Jess ran up the cellar steps and along the hall. Nick had never been so frightened!

The monster squeezed through the floorboards.
It pushed aside the boxes and followed Nick
and Jess.

Mum called from her room. "Can you be quiet
down there? I'm trying to write a scary story!"

Nick and Jess ran upstairs, screaming.
The monster crawled up
the stairs and reached
for them.

At the top of the stairs, Nick turned. He didn't want Jess and Mum to be in danger, so he would face the monster. "Stop!" he cried, holding out a shaking hand.

The monster stopped.

"We mean you no harm!" cried Nick. "Why are you after us?"

The monster held out a claw. "You dropped your pen," it said. It handed Mum's pen to Nick.

"Oh, thank you," said Nick.

"Please be quiet!" called Mum. "How can I write a scary story with all this noise?"

Nick, Jess and the monster looked at
the closed door. The monster put a claw
to its lips. "Shhh."

The monster crept back to the cellar. Nick and
Jess followed.

"See you later," said the monster, as it crawled
back through the floorboards.

"It might be fun having a monster as a friend,"
said Nick, grinning at Jess.

"Come and read my story," cried Mum from upstairs. "It's my scariest yet."

The cellar was creepy.
I didn't like it.
Jess wanted to
solve the mystery,
but I was scared.

When the monster
growled, I was
terrified.

But I decided to be brave and
face the monster. The monster
was friendly
after all!

Someone had been digging in the cellar, and I wanted to find out why.

I wasn't scared – until a huge, slimy monster poked his head out. I ran upstairs as fast as I could.

Nick was brave. He stopped and talked to the monster. Now he has a monster as a friend. He's lucky!

Ideas for reading

Written by Gillian Howell
Primary Literacy Consultant

Learning objectives: *(reading objectives correspond with Purple band; all other objectives correspond with Copper band)* read independently and with increasing fluency longer and less familiar texts; infer characters' feelings in fiction; empathise with characters and debate moral dilemmas portrayed in texts; identify features that writers use to provoke readers' reactions; use some drama strategies to explore stories or issues

Curriculum links: Citizenship

Interest words: scary, scariest, cellar, knocked, floorboards, squeezed, mystery, shovels, growl, slimy

Resources: pens and paper

Word count: 960

Getting started

- Read the title and blurb together and discuss the cover illustration. Ask the children what sort of story they think this will be and why.

- Discuss the glowing eyes and teeth with the children and ask them to predict what the monster might be like, supporting them in using adjectives to describe the creature they are picturing.

- Ask the children if they know what a cellar is and what it might be used for. Ask them to describe what it might be like down there.

Reading and responding

- Read pp2–3 together. Point out the word *scary* and ask them to find *scariest*. Ask them what *scariest* means and point out how the spelling of *scary* is changed to make *scariest*.

- As they read, ask the children to make a note of different words that mean *frightened* and *frightening*.

- At the end of p15, ask the children if they think the story is scary and why. What do they think will happen next?

- Ask the children to read to the end of the story, prompting and praising where necessary.